P9-CSC-928

TM

Let's Go, Yankees!

Yogi Berra

Illustrated by Danny Moore

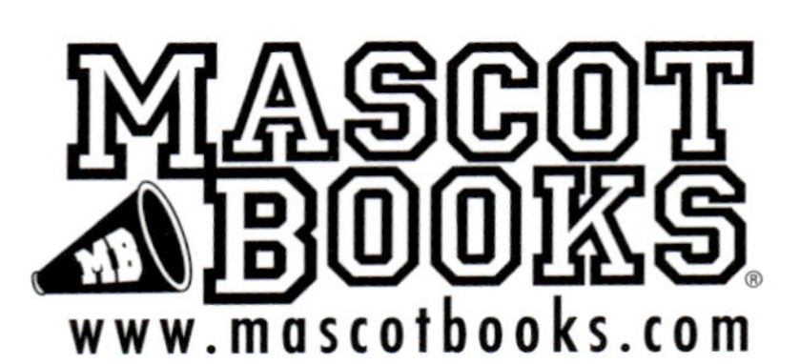

It was a beautiful day in New York City. Yankees fans were on their way to Yankee Stadium™ for a baseball game.

At the stadium station, the conductor spotted two young Yankees fans and cheered, “Let’s go, Yankees!”

The young fans walked to
Yankee Stadium. They were excited to see
"The House That Ruth Built."™

As they approached the stadium,
the young Yankees fans cheered,
“Let’s go, Yankees!”

The young Yankees fans enjoyed watching batting practice. The players wore their navy blue jerseys as they took practice swings.

The team's best hitter stepped
to the plate and said,
"Let's go, Yankees!"

After batting practice, the grounds crew quickly prepared the field for play.

As they worked, the grounds crew cheered, “Let’s go, Yankees!”

The young Yankees fans made their way to
Monument Park, where the greatest
Yankees of all time are honored.

At the Park, they ran into Yogi Berra!
Yogi signed autographs for children and
said, “Let’s go, Yankees!”

The young Yankees fans grabbed a few snacks. The smell of good food was everywhere!

As they headed back to their seats, a family cheered, "Let's go, Yankees!"

It was now time to introduce the
New York Yankees! The team was dressed
in their classic pinstriped uniforms.

As the team was announced, the players gathered on the first base line. The crowd cheered, “Let’s go, Yankees!”

“Play ball!” yelled the umpire
and the pitcher delivered the first pitch.
“Strike one!”

The pitcher turned to his teammates
and said, “Let’s go, Yankees!”

The children jumped out of their seats for the seventh inning stretch. Everyone sang "Take Me Out To The Ballgame!"™

After the song, the crowd cheered,
"Let's go, Yankees!"

With the game tied in the ninth inning, a
Yankees player hit a deep fly ball.
Home run!

The team gathered around home plate to celebrate the victory. The team cheered, "Yankees win! Yankees win!"

After the game, the young Yankees fans made their way back to the train.

As they boarded, the conductor greeted
the happy Yankees fans.
Everyone cheered “Let’s go, Yankees!”

Special thanks to:

The Berra Family
Al Santasiere

For more information about our products,
please visit us online at www.mascotbooks.com.

Mascot Books, Inc.
P.O. Box 220157
Chantilly, VA 20153-0157

ISBN: 1-932888-81-0

Printed in the United States.

www.mascotbooks.com